Postman Pat

The Secret

Story by **John Cunliffe**
Pictures by **Celia Berridge**

from the original Television designs by Ivor Wood

Hippo

Scholastic Children's Books,
7-9 Pratt Street, London NW1 OAE UK
A division of Scholastic Publications Ltd
London - New York - Toronto - Sydney - Auckland

First published in hardback by André Deutsch Limited, 1982
This edition published in the UK by Scholastic Publications Ltd, 1995

ISBN 0 590 13257 1

Printed by Mateu Cromo, S.A. Pinto (Madrid)

Typeset by Rapid

10 9 8 7 6 5 4 3 2

It was a special day for Pat. He sang as he drove along the valley. It was a happy day, too. Jess sat beside him, and twitched his whiskers.

4

"Now, young Jess, don't you give my secret away," said Pat. Jess said not one word about it.

When Pat arrived at the village post office, Mrs. Goggins was looking out for him. She was looking very pleased about something.

"Hello, Pat," she said, "there's a lot of post today!"
Who could be writing all these letters to Pat? One had a drawing of a cat on it.
The writing looked like Katy Pottage's.

"Why don't you open them?" said Mrs. Goggins.

So Pat did.

What a surprise! They were all birthday cards!

There was one from every person on his round. How did they all know that it was his birthday? Now it was no longer a secret.

"How did they know?" said Mrs. Goggins. "Well, *I* didn't tell them. Happy Birthday, Pat, and many happy returns."

Pat bought six chocolate kittens, then gathered up all his cards, and the day's letters, and went on his way.

At Greendale Farm, the twins sang "Happy Birthday to You", when Pat came in with the letters, and Mrs. Pottage joined in, too.

He showed them all his cards. Then Mrs. Pottage whisked a cloth off the table, and there was a birthday cake, with an icing-sugar post office van on it, and pink letters saying BIRTHDAY GREETINGS TO POSTMAN PAT.

There was a sugar mouse for Jess.

"But how did you know it was my birthday?" said Pat.

"We're not telling," said Mrs. Pottage. "It's a secret."

"It *was* a secret," sighed Pat. "But, all the same. . . thank you very much; it is a lovely cake."

Pat went on his way.

The church was the next stop.

"Here's something for your birthday," said the Reverend Timms. He gave Pat a Bible, bound in leather.

"That's very kind of you," said Pat, "but how did you know it was my birthday?"

"He who reads shall learn," said the Reverend.

"Oh?" said Pat, puzzled. How could the Bible tell the secret of his birthday?
Jess wondered if it was a sugar Bible.

Pat drove away, up the winding hilly roads to Thompson Ground. Mrs Thompson was looking at Pat's birthday cards when Alf came in.

"Hello, Pat," he said. "Happy birthday!"

He gave Pat a walking stick, with a curly sheep's horn for a handle.

"Thank you," said Pat, "it will be very useful, but how did you know it was my birthday?"

"Oh, you're a famous postman, you know," said Alf, smiling.

"Whatever does he mean?" thought Pat, as he waved goodbye. He was getting more and more puzzled, and his van was filling up with presents. Jess didn't like the walking stick; he thought it might poke him when he wasn't looking.

When Pat called on Granny Dryden, she gave him a woolly vest that she had knitted specially. It looked very itchy!

Miss Hubbard gave him a steering-wheel cover, made of red velvet, to keep his hands warm in winter.

At Intake Farm, George Lancaster gave Pat two dozen eggs, all different colours.

When Pat met Sam Waldron along the road with his mobile shop, Sam gave him a big box of strawberries and carton of cream.

Pat called at the village school. The children sang two songs that they had been practising, and gave Pat a big model of his van that they had made specially.

Pat gave them a chocolate kitten each, to say *thank you* for all their cards.
When he asked how they knew about his birthday, the children smiled,
pressed fingers to their lips, and said nothing.

It was time for Pat to go home. Sara would have a special birthday tea ready for him. He stopped to empty the letter-box. Peter Fogg came along on his tractor, and stopped for a chat. Pat told him about how everyone knew his birthday.

"Don't you know why?" said Peter, laughing.

"I certainly do not!" said Pat.

Peter pulled the Pencaster Gazette out of his pocket.

"Look at this," he said.

Pat was amazed. There was a big headline: HAPPY BIRTHDAY TO THE POSTMAN OF THE YEAR.

"Well," said Pat, "so that's how everyone knew. I wonder how they found out?"

"Keep it as a souvenir," said Peter.

"Thanks," said Pat, "and that surely is my last present today."

Jess wondered when *his* birthday could be. Never mind, there would be a good dinner waiting for him. That was as good as a birthday any time.

"What a strange day," said Pat. "We've finished up with a van full of letters and parcels."

And off they went home.

Jess didn't have his usual cat-nap – he wanted to keep an eye on that
sheep's horn, just in case it tried anything funny.